A NOTE TO

Congratulations on choosing the best in educational materials for your child. By selecting top-quality McGraw-Hill products, you can be assured that the concepts used in our books will reinforce and enhance the skills that are being taught in classrooms nationwide.

And what better way to get young readers excited than with Mercer Mayer's Little Critter, a character loved by children everywhere? Our First Readers offer simple and engaging stories about Little Critter that children can read on their own. Each level incorporates reading skills, colorful illustrations, and challenging activities.

Level 1 – The stories are simple and use repetitive language. Illustrations are highly supportive.
Level 2 - The stories begin to grow in complexity. Language is still repetitive, but it is mixed with more challenging vocabulary.
Level 3 - The stories are more complex. Sentences are longer and more varied.

To help your child make the most of this book, look at the first few pictures in the story and discuss what is happening. Ask your child to predict where the story is going. Then, once your child has read the story, have him or her review the word list and do the activities. This will reinforce vocabulary words from the story and build reading comprehension.

You are your child's first and most influential teacher. No one knows your child the way you do. Tailor your time together to reinforce a newly acquired skill or to overcome a temporary stumbling block. Praise your child's progress and ideas, take delight in his or her imagination, and most of all, enjoy your time together!

Library of Congress Cataloging-in-Publication Data

Mayer, Mercer, 1943-
    The mixed-up morning / by Mercer Mayer.
        p. cm. – (First readers, skills and practice)
    Summary: Little Critter's morning goes from bad to worse when he wakes up late, can't find his favorite
shirt, and misses the school bus, but his teacher knows just how to cheer him up. Includes activities.
    ISBN 1-57768-808-2
    [1. Mood (Psychology)—Fiction. 2. Schools—Fiction.] I. Title. II. Series.

PZ7.M462 Mix 2001

[E]—dc21   2001031207

McGraw-Hill
Children's Publishing

A Division of The **McGraw·Hill** Companies

Send all inquiries to:
McGraw-Hill Children's Publishing
8787 Orion Place
Columbus, OH 43240-4027

Printed in the United States of America.

1-57768-808-2

1 2 3 4 5 6 7 8 9 10 PHXBK 06 05 04 03 02 01

 A Big Tuna Trading Company, LLC/J. R. Sansevere Book

THE MIXED-UP MORNING

by Mercer Mayer

 McGraw-Hill
Children's Publishing

Columbus, Ohio

It was Monday morning.
"Time for school, Little Critter," said Mom.
"Okay, Mom," I said.
Then I fell back asleep.
Mom had to wake me up again.
It was not a good way to start the day.

I wanted to wear my
favorite green shirt.
It was dirty.
I had to wear my red one instead.

7

I wanted to have waffles for breakfast.
Little Sister ate the last one.
I had to have oatmeal instead.

9

I couldn't find my
Super Critter lunchbox.
I had to use a brown paper
bag instead.

11

I tried to catch the school bus.
I ran as fast as I could.
I was too late.
Mom had to drive me to
school instead.

13

14

I wanted to see my friends before
school started.
I could not find them.
I went to my classroom instead.

I wanted to read a book before class.
Miss Kitty asked me to help her instead.
We cleaned the classroom together.
"Thank you, Little Critter," said Miss Kitty.
That was a great way to start the day.

Word List

Read each word in the list below. Then, find it in the story. Now, make up a new sentence using the word. Say your sentence out loud.

Words I Know
school
green
shirt
red
lunchbox
bag
bus

Challenge Words
morning
asleep
again
favorite
dirty
friends
together

Proper Nouns

A proper noun names a person, place, or thing. It always begins with a capital letter. Can you find the proper nouns in the story?

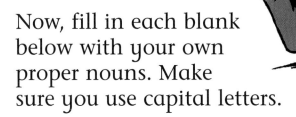

Now, fill in each blank below with your own proper nouns. Make sure you use capital letters.

Your name_____

_____

The name of a friend_____

_____

The name of your town_____

The name of your school_____

The name of a day of the week

_____

Word Decoding

When you see a big word, look for smaller words that are inside the bigger word. These smaller words will help you pronounce the bigger word.

For example, in is at the beginning of instead.

Circle each smaller word in the words below. The first one has been done for you.

Little   together

Critter   before

morning   oatmeal

favorite   Monday

Hint: Only look for small words that will help you pronounce the big word. Do not circle the on in Monday since it will not help you pronounce Monday.

Describing Words

Adjectives are words that describe nouns. They help paint a picture in your mind.

Help Little Critter get to school. Use describing words to trace a path through the maze.

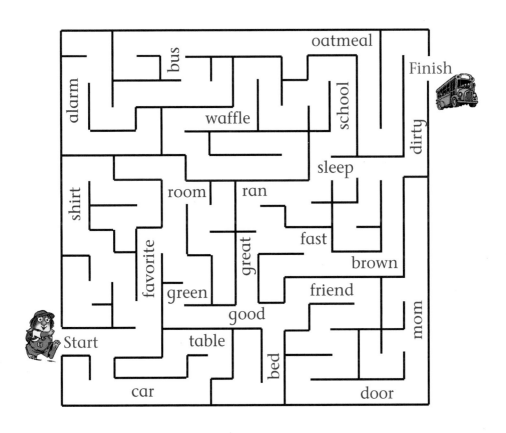

Cause and Effect

Fill in the blanks below. Try to do it without looking back at the story.

Little Sister ate the last waffle,

so_____

_____

_____

Little Critter couldn't find his Super Critter

lunchbox, so _____

_____

_____

Miss Kitty asked Little Critter to help her,

so _____

_____

_____

Vowel Sounds

In each group of words below, there is one word that does not sound the same as the other words in the group. Cross out the word that does not belong.

Short A Words

had   class

last   bed

catch   asked

Long A Words

wake   green

ate   day

late   paper

Long E Words

green   me

time   see

cleaned asleep

Answer Key

page 19
Proper Nouns

Proper Nouns from the story:
Monday
Little Critter
Mom
Little Sister
Super Critter
Miss Kitty

Other answers will vary.

page 20
Word Decoding

Little   together

Critter   before

morning   oatmeal

favorite   Monday

Parents: The circled words support the pronunciation of the larger word. Example: "Get" and "her" do not help pronounce "together," but "to" does.

page 21
Describing Words

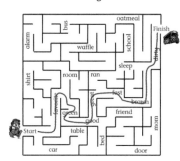

page 22
Cause and Effect

Little Sister ate the last waffle, so **Little Critter had to have oatmeal.**

Little Critter couldn't find his Super Critter lunchbox, so **he used a brown paper bag.**

Miss Kitty asked Little Critter to help her, so **he helped clean the classroom.**

page 23
Vowel Sounds

Short A Words

had   class
last   ~~bed~~
catch   asked

Long A Words

wake   ~~green~~
ate   day
late   paper

Long E Words

green   me
~~time~~   see
cleaned   asleep